CLICK!

To Ruth Haldeman and Susan Livingston,
for joining me on the journey
S. C.

To Carolyn, Alex, and Mom
J. B.

Fitzhenry & Whiteside, 195 Allstate Parkway, Markham, Ontario L3R 4T8

In the United States,
121 Harvard Avenue, Suite 2, Allston, Massachusetts 02134

www.fitzhenry.ca godwit@fitzhenry.ca

10 9 8 7 6 5 4 3 2 1

National Library of Canada Cataloguing in Publication

Crum, Shutta, 1951-
Click! / by Shutta Crum ; illustrations by John Beder.

ISBN 1-55005-074-5

I. Beder, John II. Title.

PZ7.C955Cl 2003   813'.6   C2003-902335-4

U.S. Publisher Cataloging-in-Publication Data
(Library of Congress Standards)

Crum, Shutta.
Click! / Shutta Crum ; illustrated by John Beder.—1st ed.
[   ] p. : col. ill. ; cm.
Summary: A little cub and a small hunter wander away from the safety
of their mothers to find themselves face to face.
ISBN 1-55005-074-5
1. Bears _ Fiction _ Juvenile literature.   2. Mother and child -_ Fiction _ Juvenile literature.
(1. Bears _ Fiction.   2. Mother and child -_ Fiction.)   I. Beder, John. II. Title.
[E] 21   PZ7.C776Cl 2003

Fitzhenry & Whiteside acknowledges with thanks the Canada Council for the Arts,
the Government of Canada through the Book Publishing Industry Development Program (BPIDP),
the Ontario Arts Council and the Government of Ontario through the Ontario Media Development
Corporation's Ontario Book Initiative for their support for our publishing program.

Design by Wycliffe Smith Design Inc.

Printed in Hong Kong

CLICK!

WRITTEN BY SHUTTA CRUM

ILLUSTRATED BY JOHN BEDER

Fitzhenry & Whiteside

Rest, Little One.
The daylight comes creeping,
and our deep, lovely night must go.

Mama is near.
Little stars should be sleeping
while others are waking below.

Under a blanket of snow,
a great bear sleeps,
and a small bear dreams
        close by his mother's side.

Hushed in a snow-covered house,
a great hunter sleeps,
and a small hunter dreams
close by his mother's side.

Up through the shimmering snow,
the great bear rises,
and the small bear tumbles
    down the slippery slope.
Surprise!

Up through a flurry of blankets,
the great hunter wakes,
and the small hunter tumbles
   down on the bed and laughs.
Surprise!

Striding through thawing snows,
the great bear travels,
and the small bear follows
close in his mother's tracks.

Hugging the old highway,
the great hunter speeds,
and the small hunter clings
close to his mother's back.

Back to the home of the seal,
the great bear returns,
and the small bear dips
    a paw in this new, wet world.

High on a sloping ridge,
the great hunter watches,
and the small hunter lifts
   his eyes to this new, white world.

Stalking the fish and the seal,
the great bear hunts,
and the small bear races
     birds up and down the ice.

Hidden from curious bears,
the great hunter stalks,
and the small hunter chases
birds nearby on the ice.

Under the sun's lazy stare,
a small white bear
and a small bear hunter slip – OOPS! –
and slide down an icy slope.

SURPRISE!

Click!

Into the day's sudden hush,
the great bear roars,
and the small bear hurries
    back for the long trek home.

Into the day's fading light,
the great hunter calls,
and the small hunter hurries
    back for the long ride home.

now, homeward all hunters go,
while two twinkling bears
and one old north star
brighten the way down below.

Look, Little One.
The darkness is streaming,
and our deep, lovely night's all aglow.

Mama is here.
Little stars are all gleaming,
while others are dreaming below.